The Bobbsey Twins
of Lakeport

New edition! Revised and abridged

By Laura Lee Hope

Illustrations by Pepe Gonzalez

Publishers · GROSSET & DUNLAP · New York

Look for these new
BOBBSEY TWINS® reissues:

Copyright © 1989 by Simon & Schuster, Inc. All rights reserved. Published by Grosset & Dunlap, Inc.,
a member of The Putnam & Grosset Group, New York. GROSSET & DUNLAP is a trademark of
Grosset & Dunlap, Inc. THE BOBBSEY TWINS is a registered trademark of Simon & Schuster, Inc.
Printed in the U.S.A. Published simultaneously in Canada.
Library of Congress Catalog Card Number 88-80422
ISBN 0-448-09071-6   J

Contents

■ 1 ■
The Treasure Key

"A mystery?" Nan exclaimed. "Oh, Mom, please tell us what it is!"

"Yes, Mommy," Flossie echoed, hopping excitedly from one foot to the other. "What is it?"

The four Bobbsey children followed their mother into the living room and huddled close to her as she sat down. Mary Bobbsey had just returned from the Rolling Acres Retirement Home, where she did volunteer work.

"Well," Mrs. Bobbsey began, "today at Rolling Acres I was speaking with Mrs. Marden."

"The lady who used to live in the old house next to our school?" Bert asked. His brown eyes flashed toward Nan, his twelve-year-old twin sister.

"That's right. Mrs. Marden's husband was a descendant of an ambassador to Great Britain, who had come to Lakeport when he retired. He

1

bought several acres of land and put up the house. It really was quite beautiful."

"Danny Rugg says it's haunted!" six-year-old Freddie exclaimed, sending a shudder through Flossie, his twin.

"You know Danny is always trying to scare you and Flossie," Nan said. She rumpled her sister's fluffy blond curls. "I wouldn't believe him if I were you."

"What do you think, Mom?" Bert asked.

"Just because a place is old and run-down doesn't mean that it's spooky," Mrs. Bobbsey replied. "However, it seems some valuable gifts that meant a lot to Mrs. Marden have disappeared."

"What are they, Mommy?"

"Where did she keep them?"

"Do they have anything to do with the ghost?"

The questions came so fast that Mrs. Bobbsey didn't have time to answer them. "Well, I—"

"Do they? Do they?" Freddie burst out, bringing even more questions from the others.

"Whoa, slow down, everybody. If you'll listen, I'll tell you all about it." Mrs. Bobbsey brushed back a stray dark hair.

"We're sorry, Mom," Nan apologized. "Now, let Mother talk, okay?" she chided the younger children.

When they were quiet again, Mrs. Bobbsey

2

went on with her story. "When Old Mr. Marden left England, the royal family presented him with two special gifts. One was a beautiful cameo brooch surrounded by diamonds."

"What's a cameo?" Flossie asked.

"It's a very unusual gemstone," her mother explained, "which is made by carving a shell or precious stone that has layers of different colors. When the carving is done, a figure of one color stands out against the background of another color."

"Mm, that sounds pretty," Nan commented.

"The other thing Mrs. Marden has lost is a collection of rare obsidional coins."

"What are obsid'nal coins?" Freddie asked, furrowing his brow.

"Ob-sid-i-o-nal," his older brother corrected. He went to a bookshelf and picked out a thick volume. "According to this," Bert said, flipping to an entry, "they're also called siege pieces, or coins of necessity. They were made by towns in Europe that were under attack, in order to pay the defending troops."

"How old are they, son?" Richard Bobbsey, a tall athletic-looking man, strode into the room. He had finished work early at the lumberyard he owned.

"Hi, Daddy." Flossie darted toward her father while Bert displayed some pictures of the coins.

"These are from the sixteenth and seventeenth centuries," Bert said.

"And look, the coins are four-sided!" Nan said.

"Let me see." Freddie eased in front of her and smiled. "They look like itty-bitty boxes!"

"'The coins were made from any material the authorities could find,'" Bert read on, "'melted-down statues and church silver. Often they were irregularly shaped.'"

"I'd love to see some coins like that," Nan said."

"Well, you will," her mother said with a sigh, "if you can locate Mrs. Marden's. She said she put hers away in a very safe place in the old house, but now she can't remember where. Sometimes when people get old, their memory begins to fail."

"That's a shame," Mr. Bobbsey remarked. "Has she been back to the house since the school bought it?"

"No. She moved right into Rolling Acres afterward, and that's where she has been ever since." A sad smile played across Mrs. Bobbsey's face. "Poor Mrs. Marden. Her husband died a few years ago, so she has no one to help her. But I told her how much you all enjoy solving mysteries."

The four Bobbsey children hung on every word as their mother finished speaking. "She'd

4

like you to hunt for the missing heirlooms!"

"I can't wait!" Bert said gleefully.

"D-do we have to go into that spooky house?" Flossie said with a shiver.

"It's probably locked," Nan said, "but maybe our principal, Mr. Tetlow, will give us a key."

"We can see him on Monday," Bert agreed.

"Mommy, did you ask Mrs. Marden about a ghost in the house?" Flossie asked, snuggling close to her mother.

"No, I didn't, pumpkin."

As Mrs. Bobbsey spoke, Dinah Johnson, the family's beloved housekeeper, stood in the doorway. Her dark velvety eyes sparkled under thick lashes.

"Now, who is ready for a piece of my ghost-chiffon pie?" she asked, trying to keep a straight face.

"Ghost chiffon?" Bert repeated quizzically.

"Mm-hmm. When you eat it, it disappears!" Dinah said.

Her mocha-brown lips broke into a wide grin as the children raced into the kitchen. The minute Flossie saw Dinah's creamy lemon-chiffon pie she forgot her fear of the Marden house.

By Monday, Flossie was ready to start the search. On the way to school the twins met Bert and Nan's best friends. Charlie Mason was about

Bert's height and had dark hair and brown eyes. Nellie Parks, Nan's friend, was a pretty blond girl with dazzling blue eyes.

"Hi, everybody!" Nellie called as the six children met at the corner.

"Hello, Nell," Flossie replied. "We're going to solve a mystery!"

"You are?" Nellie asked, her eyes widening with interest. "What's it about?"

Bert and Nan took turns telling their friends the story of Mrs. Marden and the valuable cameo and coins that she had misplaced.

"Whew!" Charlie exclaimed. "That *is* a mystery! Are you going to search the old house?"

"Yes," Bert replied. "Would you and Nellie like to help us?"

The children accepted instantly. They discussed the mystery all the way to school.

Then Charlie asked, "When are you going to talk to Mr. Tetlow?"

"Right after school," Bert said, "so let's meet in the hall. Okay?"

"Okay. See you later."

The day seemed very long. From where Nan sat in her homeroom, next to a window overlooking the school lawn, she could see the deserted Marden house. It was a large three-story frame building, which at one time had been

7

painted white. Now the paint was worn and chipped. The once-green shutters hung at crazy angles. Two of the windows on the second floor had been broken, and dangling from one of them was a torn window shade.

"Where could Mrs. Marden have hidden the cameo and coins?" Nan mused. "If she left them in a cupboard or closet, someone may have already found them and taken them away. She'll be very upset if she doesn't get her things back."

When the afternoon classes finally ended, Nan and Bert hurried to the principal's office.

"Is Mr. Tetlow expecting you?" the school secretary inquired.

Nan spoke up. "No, but my brother and I have a question we'd like to ask him—if he isn't too busy, that is."

The young woman disappeared into the principal's private office and returned in a few minutes. "Mr. Tetlow says to come in," she announced from the doorway.

He was seated behind his large paper-filled desk, and smiled as the twins entered. "I'm glad to see you, Nan and Bert. What can I do for you today?"

"We'd like you to help us solve a mystery," Nan said boldly as Mr. Tetlow leaned back in his chair.

He pushed his glasses to the top of his head.

"Well, that sounds very interesting. What kind of a mystery is it?"

Quickly Bert explained about Mrs. Marden and the fact that she could not remember where she had hidden the royal presents.

"You know, don't you, that the old house is going to be torn down?" Mr. Tetlow responded.

The twins shook their heads.

"Well, it is, and very soon, I'm afraid."

Bert and Nan looked at each other. "Then we've just got to investigate it," Bert said. "I mean, with your permission, sir."

Mr. Tetlow explained that although all the furniture had been taken out of the house, the school authorities had decided to keep it locked.

"Sometimes old houses are ransacked. Good wood, plumbing fixtures, and lighting fixtures can be sold," the principal said. "But I have no objection if you want to look for Mrs. Marden's property. You've always been very responsible. I'll let you have our extra key for a little while. Just be sure to bring it to school each day in case anyone needs to get into the house. I have a key, but I might not be available when you need it."

Nan's eyes were shining. "Thank you, Mr. Tetlow. We'll be very careful," she said, "and we'll make sure we lock the house when we leave."

The friendly gray-haired man opened a desk

drawer and took out a large old-fashioned key. "This is it," he said. "I'll mark it for you."

As Nan and Bert watched, Mr. Tetlow tied a white tag to the key. In tiny letters he wrote on the tag: "Marden House, property of Lakeport School Board." Then he handed it to Bert.

"Good luck. I hope you find Mrs. Marden's valuables for her."

When Bert and Nan left the principal's office, they found Charlie and Nellie waiting in the hall.

"What did he say?" Nellie asked immediately.

Bert grinned and pulled the big key out of his pocket.

"Fantastic!" Charlie exclaimed.

As the four children started toward the school entrance, a boy stepped from a nearby class-room. He was taller and heavier than Bert and Charlie, and his freckled face was twisted in an evil smirk.

"Danny Rugg!" Nellie cried. "Have you been spying on us?"

The boy grunted scornfully. "I've got better things to do than spy on you. But you'd better keep out of that old house. Ghosts float in and out of the broken windows upstairs!" He leapt toward Nellie, making her shriek.

◾ 2 ◾
Starting the Search

"What makes you so sure the house is haunted?" Nan asked Danny.

"I saw the ghosts myself, okay?" The boy sauntered away, calling back over his shoulder, "Don't say I didn't warn you!"

"He doesn't want us to find Mrs. Marden's things, that's all," Nan declared angrily.

Bert agreed. "Let's go inside the house and look around."

"Yeah, let's," Charlie said. "Forget about Danny."

Taking the lead, Bert headed for the deserted old mansion. As he put the key in the lock, he heard a giggle from around the corner of the porch. Freddie and Flossie stuck their heads out.

"We waited for you," Freddie announced. "Flossie and I want to go inside the haunted house too!"

"Come on, then," Nan said as Bert turned the key.

The door creaked a little, then opened on a wide center hall. The six children stepped inside. Although they moved slowly, their footsteps sounded loud and hollow in the empty space.

Flossie stayed close to her older sister as they peered around. "Are you okay?" Nan asked the little girl. Flossie said yes but felt a lump in her throat.

At one side of the hall was a broad, sweeping stairway. The steps were littered with bits of fallen plaster, and the paper that covered the walls was stained and peeling in places.

"Ooh, it *is* sort of spooky!" Nellie remarked, catching a sneeze.

"And very dusty," Nan said. She ran a finger across a windowsill and held it up to show the grime on her skin.

There were four closed doors, two on each side of the hall. Gingerly the children pulled back the first one on the left. It led to the living room, which had a large fireplace at the far end.

The playmates crossed the hall and opened the door there. "This must have been the dining room," Nan said, seeing built-in cupboards in two corners of the room.

"And this was the library," Bert guessed as

they went into the room behind the living room. Two walls contained bookshelves that extended almost to the ceiling.

Freddie, in the meantime, had gone to the fourth door. He tugged at the handle, which was stiffer than the others. "Come and help me, Floss," he called out.

The little twin scampered toward him along with the others.

"Here, let me do that," Bert said. "Stand back, everyone." He grasped the handle with both hands and yanked hard.

Instantly the door swung free, revealing a small corridor and another room at the end of it, which appeared to be the kitchen. A fireplace took up one end of the room almost entirely but was blocked by a pile of logs.

"The fireplace is huge!" Charlie exclaimed as they stood inside the kitchen.

"That's because people used to cook in fireplaces," Nan said.

"Let's see what's upstairs," Bert proposed.

There was a narrow flight of stairs leading from the kitchen, and the children crept up carefully. On the second floor they found five more rooms. As in the others, paper was falling from the walls in strips. Closet doors stood open, and torn window shades hung unevenly over the windows.

"There aren't very many places to search," Nan sighed. "Just as Mr. Tetlow said, everything has been cleared out."

Bert suggested, "We could break up into teams—"

A sudden loud *bang* shattered the stillness. Flossie screamed. "It's the ghost!" she cried, clinging to her sister.

Nellie gulped. "What *was* that?"

Bert walked to a window and gazed outside. The others gathered behind him.

"There's your ghost, Floss." He laughed, pointing to a loose shutter.

As they watched, a gust of wind struck the shutter hard and slammed it against the side of the house.

Flossie's lip quivered. "I want to go home!" she pleaded.

"It's getting late anyway," Nan said, taking her sister's hand. "We'll come back some other time."

At breakfast the next morning Nan said she wanted to see Mrs. Marden and ask her a few questions.

"Can I—I mean, may I—go with you?" Flossie asked. "Please, please?"

"Sure," Nan said.

"I'm going out that way this afternoon," their

14

mother said. "If you like, I can drop you both off at Rolling Acres."

The boys had made other plans, but Mrs. Bobbsey said she would meet Nan and Flossie at the end of the school day. When the dismissal bell rang that afternoon, the girls took their coats and ran outside, where their mother was waiting.

"Dinah baked some cookies for Mrs. Marden," she said as Nan and Flossie got into the car.

"Yum-meee," the older replied, opening the box.

Flossie dipped her chubby finger inside.

"They're not for us," Nan said, and pushed the lid down again.

"No, but here are some that are," said Mrs. Bobbsey, passing a small plastic bag to Nan.

Nan and Flossie were munching on their last cookies as they pulled up in front of a large comfortable-looking building with a gently sloping lawn and budding daffodils.

"I'll be back in about an hour to pick you girls up," Mrs. Bobbsey said.

Flossie and Nan waved good-bye to their mother as they ran up the stone walk to the front door. The receptionist phoned Mrs. Marden, and soon the elderly woman met them in a large sitting room. Nan introduced herself and Flossie.

"It's very nice of you to come see me," Mrs. Marden said, giving the children a hug.

"Dinah sent you some cookies," Nan said. As she handed over the box, Flossie's eyes traveled after it longingly.

"Why, thank you, dear," Mrs. Marden said, peeking at the assorted contents. "Would you like one?" she asked.

Nan declined politely and glared at Flossie, who took one of the chocolate-chip cookies. Then Flossie blurted out, "Do you remember where you hid the pin and the coins?"

Mrs. Marden shook her head gravely.

"Don't be sad," Flossie said. "I know a song that will make you happy. I made it up myself."

"You did?"

The woman's face brightened as Flossie sang a song about a cricket. It ended, "And the cricket on your hearth goes *chirp, chirp, chirp!*"

"That's it!" Mrs. Marden exclaimed. "The hearth! It has something to do with my lost treasure!"

The Bobbsey girls tingled with excitement. "Can you think of anything more?" Nan asked.

Mrs. Marden drew her lips together in a thin line. "I'm sorry, my dear. It's just no use."

"Don't worry, Mrs. Marden," Nan said. "We won't give up looking."

16

That evening Nan and Flossie described their visit to Rolling Acres. When they said how excited Mrs. Marden had been at the mention of a hearth, Bert snapped his fingers.

"Maybe the treasure is hidden under the hearth of one of the fireplaces in the house! There could be a stone that lifts out!" he reasoned.

"There are lots of fireplaces in that house," Freddie recalled.

"Let's take a look tomorrow after school," Nan suggested.

But the next afternoon Freddie and Flossie went home to play with some of their friends.

"Nell and I have to go to a meeting," Nan told Bert, "but I can go to the Marden house later."

The school was planning to add a new gymnasium, and the students were organizing different activities to raise money for modern equipment. Nan and Nellie were members of one of the committees.

"Okay," Bert agreed. "I'll hang around until you're ready."

He wandered out into the schoolyard as Charlie Mason came running up.

"Are you going to search the Marden house again?" he asked hurriedly.

"Yes," said Bert. "I'm just waiting for Nan."

"Well, I have to go home now. I have a dentist's appointment," Charlie explained.

"If we don't find anything this trip," Bert promised, "we can all go back tomorrow."

In a little while Nan came out of the school building alone. When she heard about Charlie, she said, "Nell couldn't stay either, so I guess it's just you and me this time."

As the twin detectives approached the old house, Bert took the big iron key from his pocket. "Maybe we should split up the rooms to save time," he said, opening the door.

Nan nodded. "I'll take the right side of the first floor and you take the left. If we don't find anything, then we can go upstairs together."

Bert walked into the old living room. The hearth and the space around the opening were trimmed with blue-and-white tiles. On each was a picture of an animal or a delicate flower.

"I wonder if there's a loose one," he murmured. He knelt down and carefully ran his fingers over every tile on the hearth. Several were cracked, but all of them fit solidly together.

Next he examined the tiles on both sides of the fireplace. He took a small penknife from his pocket and tapped them, looking for some sign of tampering, but found none.

Then he peered up into the fireplace. There

was only a small flue and no place to hide anything. Rubbing his chin, Bert paced back and forth. He felt around the baseboard and window frames. Everything was solid.

He sighed and went into the library. Once more he examined the hearth. This one was made of bricks, but like the tiles, they were set firmly and did not move under Bert's touch. Now he scanned each of the empty bookshelves from top to bottom.

"Well, so much for this room," he thought, convinced that the treasure was hidden elsewhere.

Nan, in the meantime, had entered the dining room and gone immediately to the old fireplace. It was paneled in wood. She had tapped each panel and tried to move it, but, like her brother, she had no success.

She went to the corner cupboards and traced her fingers along the wooden backs and sides. Again nothing budged. Curiosity sent her down the hall and into the small passage that led to the kitchen. As she opened the door, she saw a trapdoor in front of the huge fireplace slowly closing!

"Bert!" Nan screamed.

■ 3 ■

Trapped!

Bert dashed into the room. "What's the matter?" he asked anxiously.

Nan pointed to the floor. "Th-there's a trapdoor right there, and somebody just went through it!" she cried.

Her brother ran forward. "You're right, Nan!" he said. "I can see an outline, but there's no way to open it from this side!"

"Wh-who do you suppose it was?" Nan continued, still trembling.

"Danny Rugg. He warned us about coming to the house."

"I suppose it was Danny," Nan said. "Let's not tell Freddie and Flossie, though. They might worry."

So when Bert and Nan arrived home, they said nothing to the younger twins about the trapdoor. Bert, however, continued to puzzle over the episode.

When he saw Danny Rugg the next day, he said abruptly, "Don't think you scared Nan and me yesterday!"

"What are you talking about?" Danny replied, clearly annoyed. "I didn't try to scare you!"

"Come on, Danny!" Bert protested. "You know you were in the Marden house. You went through that trapdoor in the kitchen yesterday afternoon."

"I don't know anything about a trapdoor." Then Danny grinned slyly. "But remember, I told you the house was haunted. Maybe you saw the ghost!"

"What ghost?" Bert retaliated. "You know there's no such thing!"

"Oh, no?" Danny walked away, whistling.

When Bert and Nan left their homeroom at the end of the day, Bert told his sister what Danny had said. Both were reluctantly convinced that the bully had not been in the house. But if he hadn't, who had?

"If the person had a right to be there," Nan said, "he wouldn't have run away because of us."

"Exactly," her brother said.

As they talked, they reached the outside door, where a group of children was standing nearby. They seemed to be looking at something on the ground.

Bert went up to Charlie, who was at the fringe of the group. "What's going on?" he asked.

"They're pouring concrete for the new driveway," the boy answered.

Charlie and the twins walked around to the other side, where the concrete mixer churned noisily.

"How long does it take for concrete to harden?" Charlie shouted to Bert.

"I don't know, but if you step in it when it's wet, your footprint will stay there forever."

In the meantime, Freddie and Flossie also were getting ready to leave school. Freddie tapped his twin on the arm. "You're it!" He giggled, careening down the hall.

By this time there were only a few children left in the building and the hall was empty. Flossie ran after Freddie and tagged him. "Now you're it!" she teased, running away.

Freddie stepped into an empty classroom. When Flossie turned around, he was nowhere in sight, which confused her. She began to tiptoe back down the hall.

As she reached the empty classroom, Freddie suddenly jumped out at her. Flossie shrieked, then ran toward the front door. "You can't catch me!"

Outside the building Bert saw her leap down the steps. However, she was looking back and did not notice what was being done to the driveway. Bert called to her, but it was too late.

Flossie ran right into the soft cement! The onlookers gasped as the girl's little feet sank in the gooey mire.

"Help!" she cried.

"Stand still!" Nan ordered.

Flossie was too agitated to stand still. She tried to take a step. But the cement held fast to the shoes, making her feet pop out of them and into the sticky goo. Now she was really trapped—in her socks! She looked at the other children in desperation and wept.

"Wait a minute, Flossie!" Bert said. "We'll get you out."

"Here are some boards," Charlie called. He ran to a pile of thin wood strips and laid them together across the driveway near Flossie. "Can you reach them?"

The little girl replied by slipping out of her socks and stepping from the wet cement onto the wood. Slowly she made her way across until she reached safe ground. Then Bert crawled onto the makeshift bridge and pulled out her shoes and socks.

"It was just like peanut butter," Flossie told Nan as a workman hurried toward them.

"Are you all right?" he asked, staring at the twin's bare feet.

Flossie wiggled her toes. "Yes, sir. But I'm very sorry. I didn't know it was soft."

The man patted her on the head. "Don't worry about it. I can smooth over the cement."

Bert, in the meantime, had scraped enough of it off her shoes so she could wear them home. When they reached the front door, he picked Flossie up and carried her into the kitchen.

"What on earth—" Mrs. Bobbsey said, gaping at her daughter.

The children quickly explained.

"Well, I was planning to get you a pair of new shoes anyway, so we'll go downtown tomorrow. I'll pick you and Freddie up at school."

Flossie loved to go shopping with her mother. Freddie didn't know whether he did or not.

"Oh, come on, Freddie," his twin pleaded. "We'll ride the escater."

Her mother's puzzled expression made Nan laugh. "I think she means 'escalator,' Mom."

"That's what I said," Flossie insisted. "The stairs that go up and down by themselves."

The next afternoon when they arrived at Taylor's Department Store, the twins were overwhelmed by all the things in the windows. There was a large display of dolls in one of them. In the corner was a little white picket fence with a toy barn inside. Dolls dressed as farmers and their helpers were pitching hay, milking cows, and feeding tiny chickens.

"Isn't it bee-yoo-ti-ful?" Flossie exclaimed in delight.

"I like this side better," Freddie said. He was admiring a little airplane hangar where toy planes zoomed through the air, and tiny soldiers in Air Force uniforms looked on from the ground.

"Let's go," Mrs. Bobbsey said, urging the twins into the store. "You can see the toys later."

They made their way to the third floor, where Flossie was soon fitted with a brand-new pair of loafers.

"I have to go to the housewares department for Dinah," Mrs. Bobbsey said, leading them past a counter of doll clothes. "But first, maybe you'd like to look around here."

"My dollies do need some new clothes," Flossie said brightly.

Freddie was not interested in his sister's dolls. So while Flossie and his mother were busy, he left them at the counter and wandered toward the escalator. Many people were riding up on it, but he saw no way of going down.

"I guess I have to walk down the stairs,"

he told himself. "I'll do that and ride up again while Mommy and Flossie are looking at those dolls. Mommy won't even know I'm gone."

Freddie noticed a door marked "Stairway." He scurried down two flights and then one more. When he reached the bottom, he found himself in the basement of the store.

A little train was going around and around on a track. Bells were ringing, and signals were flashing. He walked over to the display and watched in fascination. Then he moved on to an area that had small model automobiles.

"How about a ride?" a salesman asked.

"Really?" Freddie replied eagerly.

"Sure!" The man showed him how to operate the small vehicle, and soon Freddie was riding around the cleared floor space.

When he climbed out of the car, he thought it must be time to go back upstairs.

"Let's see," he said to himself. "I think the moving stairs are over here." But Freddie was hopelessly mixed up. He couldn't find either the stairway or the escalator.

Like the little train, he also went around and around until he came to a doorway that connected to another part of the basement. It looked like a gigantic storage room. In a well-lit corner at one end a man sat at a desk checking off items in a large ledger.

Freddie started toward him. "Can you tell me how to get up to the third floor?"

But the man was so busy he didn't hear the question. He closed his book and walked through the doorway behind him.

"Mister?" Freddie called, trailing after him, but it was no use.

Pulling the door shut, the boy saw the clerk disappear into another exit. As he did, a big overhead door slid down and Freddie heard a latch fall into place.

Although the room was warm, a nervous chill went through his small frame. He was alone in a large room lined with paper cartons and wooden boxes.

Freddie collapsed on a pile of soft packing material and let out a sigh. In a few minutes his eyes closed, his head drooped forward, and he was fast asleep.

Back at school, Bert and Charlie were waiting for Nan and Nellie to come outside. Bert had told his friend about the trapdoor in the kitchen of the old Marden house.

"Nan and I can't figure out how anyone got inside to open it," Bert said.

Charlie smiled. "I wouldn't trust Danny Rugg

28

even if he did say he wasn't there. Maybe he followed you and Nan when you weren't looking and sneaked down into the cellar."

At this moment Nan and Nellie emerged from the building. "I'm so excited," Nellie exclaimed. "I can't wait to look through that house again. Maybe today we'll find the lost treasure!"

Since Bert and Nan had thoroughly explored the first floor, the four children went upstairs. Each of them took a bedroom and searched it carefully. As before, they paid particular attention to the fireplaces, but discovered nothing.

Nellie finished her room first and went into the fifth bedroom. Suddenly she called to the others, "Come in here! I think there's something on the closet shelf!"

Nan, Bert, and Charlie ran to her side. By standing on tiptoe and craning their necks, they were able to see a small package in the far corner of the closet shelf.

"Nan, you're the lightest," Bert said. "I'll boost you up so you can get it."

He bent over and let her climb onto his back. She was barely able to reach the package and work it forward with the tips of her fingers.

"Oh, I just know it's the cameo and coins!" Nellie cried as Nan stepped down.

Her hands shaking in anticipation, Nan undid the brown paper.

■ 4 ■
The Prowler

When the children saw the contents, they groaned in disappointment. Sitting on the paper were four old-fashioned casters for chair legs!

"I was sure I had found the treasure!" Nellie said as she wrapped up the casters again and replaced them on the closet shelf.

"There's still the attic," Nan said almost cheerfully.

"Come on!" Charlie exclaimed.

The attic stairs were narrow, rickety, and very winding. The children had to be extra careful climbing them. When they reached the top, they stood quietly for a moment. There was a window at each end of the large room, which let in a small amount of light. The place looked as if it had been cleared out some time before. The floor was covered with dust, and the only thing left was a trunk under one of the eaves.

It was dark under the eaves, so the two boys dragged the old chest to the middle of the room. The catch was rusty, but Charlie managed to pry it open. He pulled up the lid.

Inside was an empty tray with a few stray buttons in it. Bert lifted the tray hastily to look underneath. He was not too surprised to find layers of musty-smelling old-fashioned dresses.

Nan ran her hand around the edges of the trunk. "There's no box here," she said, poking the dresses. "Now what?"

"It's getting dark," Nellie remarked. "I think we ought to go home."

"But we'll come back Monday," Nan agreed. "We just have to."

She led the way down the narrow stairs and had almost reached the bottom when she turned to say something to Nellie, who was behind her.

Instantly Nan pitched headfirst onto the floor! She lay very still.

"Nan!" Nellie wailed, flying down the last few steps to her friend.

Bert and Charlie leapt after her. "The bottom step is missing!" Bert exclaimed. "That's why Nan fell!"

His twin was pale and quiet. "She's really knocked out!" Nellie said. "I'll run over to the school and get some water."

She was gone and back in a flash, with a cup of water in her hand. By this time Nan was sitting up, but she was still groggy.

"Thank you, Nell," she said faintly, taking a sip of the water. "I feel all right now."

Bert and Charlie each took one of her arms and helped her down the stairs to the front door. As they reached the yard, Danny Rugg sprinted toward them.

"What happened?" he greeted them.

"As if you didn't know!" Bert said. "You sneaked in here behind us and took that step out so one of us would fall!"

"I don't know what you're talking about," Danny growled. He gave Bert a hard shove that made the boy almost lose his balance.

Bert doubled up his fist and punched Danny on the shoulder. Danny hit back, striking his attacker on the side of the face. In another minute the two were rolling on the ground.

At this point Mr. Tetlow ran out of the school. "Bert and Danny! Stop that fighting at once!"

The boys struggled to their feet, still glaring at each other.

"Now, I want to know what this is about!" Mr. Tetlow commanded sternly. "Bert?"

"Nan just had a bad fall in the Marden house. Someone must've taken out a step while we were

33

in the attic. I think *he* did it!" Bert pointed to Danny.

"Why would I do that?" the other boy whined. "I was just standing here, and he hit me!"

As Bert started to object, they heard the back door of the old house close. Next they saw a man's figure dash across the backyard and disappear through the hedges. But when they ran after him, they found no trace of anyone.

"So somebody else was in the house," the principal said, looking at Bert.

The boy hung his head. "I'm sorry, Danny. I guess I did make a mistake," he said contritely.

"Okay," Danny barked, "but don't always blame me for everything!"

Mr. Tetlow returned to school, and he had the twins come to his office. "I want to hear about your investigation."

After Bert and Nan told him again about the missing step and then about the trapdoor, the man reached for the telephone on his desk.

"I think it's time to report the whole business to the police. If you see anything else suspicious, tell me at once."

Charlie and Nellie were waiting for the twins as they left the school. All the way home the four friends chatted excitedly.

"This is getting to be more and more mysterious!" Nellie said.

"You can say that again," Nan remarked.

When at last she and Bert reached their house, they were surprised to find it in an uproar. "Freddie is lost!" Flossie sobbed to her brother and sister.

"What happened, Mom?" Nan asked, stooping to hug the little girl.

Mrs. Bobbsey explained how Freddie had vanished while she and Flossie were looking at doll clothes. "We couldn't find him anywhere!"

Flossie nodded sadly. "All the people in the store were looking for him."

"And now your father and the police are, too," her mother said.

As she spoke, the front door opened and Mr. Bobbsey walked in. He sank wearily into a chair.

"The police will find him soon," he said, trying to sound optimistic.

At that very moment Freddie awakened in the shipping room of the department store. But it was dark, and for an instant he could not remember where he was.

"Uh-oh," he thought. "I'd better go upstairs or Mommy will be worried about me."

He got to his feet and stepped forward. He bumped into a big box. Then he turned in the opposite direction and stumbled over a barrel.

"Let me out!" the little boy yelled.

But no one came.

Suddenly something soft rubbed against his leg and Freddie gasped. He stood still, listening to the silence and then finally a low purr.

"It's a kitty!" he cried joyfully. "Here, kitty." He picked up the cat, which cuddled against his small shoulder.

Confidently the little boy ran his hand along the wall until he came to a door. He turned the knob and stepped into the room where he had been earlier. It was dimly lit now. Still clutching the cat, he crossed to the second door and found himself in the mechanical-toy department. This room was very dim, too. The counters were draped with long ghostly white cloths. Freddie walked over to the model automobiles, but they were all locked. As he stepped back, however, he tripped against a robot. Its metal head was mounted on a spring, and it began to move back and forth!

Freddie shrieked in fright.

The next moment he heard footsteps overhead, and someone calling, "Who's there?" It was a man's voice, and it sounded rough and harsh. Freddie was afraid to answer.

After a few minutes there were loud, heavy steps on the stairway. The little boy crouched nervously behind a counter and peered out.

▪ 5 ▪
Cat Tales

Freddie could see the tiny glow of a flashlight and the man who was carrying it. He was bald with a ruff of white hair around his head, and his face had a soft, kind expression.

"Must have been the cat," he muttered under his breath. "Here, kitty, kitty, kitty."

"Meow!" replied the cat in Freddie's arms.

Quickly the man flashed his light around until the beam fell on Freddie. "Well, well. How did you get in here?" he asked, smiling and frowning at the same time.

Sheepishly Freddie stepped from behind the counter. "I guess I'm lost. I want my mother," he said with a little catch in his voice.

"You must be the little boy they were looking for this afternoon," the man said.

Freddie shrugged. "I was just looking at the toys, then I went in that room over there. It was

37

very warm and I fell asleep. Do you own this store?"

"No." The man chuckled. "I'm Ryan, the night watchman, and you must be Richard Bobbsey's little boy, Freddie."

"Yes, I am, Mr. Ryan. May I go home now?"

"I'm going to call your family right away. They'll be mighty glad to know you're here."

The night watchman led the way up the stairs to the main floor of the store. Freddie followed, still holding the friendly black cat in his arms.

At the Bobbsey home his father had received a report from the police that they had not found Freddie but were about to broadcast an appeal over the local radio.

Mr. Bobbsey rose slowly from his chair. "Come on, Bert," he said. "Let's scout the neighborhood again."

At that moment the telephone rang. Nan sprang to answer it.

Mr. and Mrs. Bobbsey, Bert, and Flossie listened breathlessly as Nan said hello.

"Freddie!" she cried out. "Where are you? . . . What? . . . We'll be right down!"

Nan hung up the receiver, her face radiant. "He's been at the department store this whole time!"

"Oh, thank goodness!" Mrs. Bobbsey cried.

The whole family hurried into their van, and

Mr. Bobbsey drove to the store. Freddie and the watchman were standing outside. The small black cat was still being cuddled in Freddie's arms.

"Am I glad to see you!" Freddie exclaimed.

Mr. Bobbsey threw his arms around the little boy. "You really gave us quite a scare," he said.

"I'm sorry, Daddy."

"We're just happy we found you," his mother added, giving him a squeeze. "Now, put the cat down and hop into the van."

Freddie hesitated.

"Do as your mother says," Richard Bobbsey said.

"Oh, no, Daddy," Freddie resisted. "The cat is the one who found me! He's my friend!"

Mr. Ryan laughed. "That's right. They've become good pals. I told Freddie he could keep the little fellow if you and your wife have no objection."

Mrs. Bobbsey looked at her husband. "We can't very well turn down a rescuer," she said.

"Hooray!" Freddie exclaimed.

After his parents thanked the watchman for looking after the boy, Freddie waved good-bye and climbed in beside his father. On the way home he told his story of being locked in the big store.

"Weren't you scared?" Flossie asked her twin.

Freddie admitted that it was spooky for a while. "But then the kitty came along and I wasn't alone anymore!"

"I've just made up a poem about it," Bert said.

Freddie ran off, and down he sat,
A meow woke him up, and there was a cat!

The Bobbseys laughed at the rhyme. When they reached home, Dinah greeted them at the door. "I bet you're real hungry," she said to Freddie. "Everyone was too worried to eat around here. But if you're ready now, I'll put dinner on the table."

"Thank you, Dinah," Mrs. Bobbsey said.

Later, between bites of crisp fried chicken, Flossie asked, "What's the kitty's name?"

"Mr. Ryan just called him kitty," Freddie explained.

"Maybe we should call him Taylor after the store," Nan suggested.

"Taylor?" Flossie wrinkled her nose in disapproval.

"I know," Freddie said. "How about Snoop?"

Flossie giggled. "Because he was snooping around the store and found you!"

The boy crowed triumphantly, bringing a round of applause from everyone.

The next morning was sunny and breezy. Mr. Bobbsey came into the yard where the twins were playing. "How would you like to fly some kites?" he asked.

"Oh, Dad, that would be super!" Nan cried.

"I'll show you how to build them," Mr. Bobbsey offered. "The easiest kind to make is the two-stick. There's a bundle of laths in the garage. Get those, will you, Bert?"

He instructed Freddie and the girls to bring a sharp knife, some glue, paste, and a roll of strong cord. "We'll need some paper, too."

Dinah, who was standing on the back porch, heard him. "We have red and green crepe paper left over from Christmas, if that's all right."

"Great," Mr. Bobbsey said, sending Nan to fetch it.

After all the supplies were on the picnic table, Mr. Bobbsey picked up the laths. "These are just about the right thickness," he said. "For each kite, we'll have to cut two sticks. One should be twenty-six inches long for the spine—the vertical stick—and the cross stick should be twenty-two inches long. Any questions?"

"I don't have any," Bert said, taking a pencil and ruler. Neither did anyone else.

In a little while the twins finished the first

41

step. Their father showed them how to notch a groove in the end of each stick.

"Next, you measure seven inches from one end of the longer stick and put a big pencil mark. Then glue the sticks together exactly at right angles, and center the cross stick right over the pencil mark you made."

At first Freddie and Flossie had trouble putting their sticks together. But Nan and Bert helped them. As soon as the glue was dry, they followed their father's directions and securely bound the joint with cord.

"Now comes the frame," Mr. Bobbsey said. He showed the children how to tie the end of a piece of cord to the top of the spine, then carry it around the frame through the grooves.

Finally the children cut and pasted the crepe paper onto the frames.

"I love mine!" Flossie exclaimed.

"We still have to make the bridle," her father said. He took Flossie's kite and fastened two lengths of string to the ends of the sticks and tied them in the middle. "Do you see where the bridles cross each other?"

"Yes," Flossie said as the other children watched.

"You tie this piece of string right there," Mr. Bobbsey instructed. He cut another piece about five feet long and handed it to her. "This is the leader. Whenever you want to fly your kite, just attach the rest of your cord to it."

"This is 'citing!" Flossie said.

"Let's take our kites to Roscoe's field," Bert proposed.

Old Mr. Roscoe lived in a small house near the Bobbseys'. The field next to his house was no longer cultivated, and he allowed the children to play there as much as they wanted.

"But our kites don't have any tails!" Freddie observed. "I want a tail on mine!" Snoop, who was walking beside him, meowed.

"I know how to make that," Bert spoke up. "You go ahead. I'll bring everything to the field."

In a little while Bert and his mother joined the group. The boy cut a fifteen-foot piece of cord, then strips of crepe paper, which he pleated and tied together with the cord. The other children did the same, and soon four kites with brightly colored tails lay on the ground.

"Do I have to run with it until it goes up?" Freddie asked his father.

"If the kite's right, all you have to do is hold it up. The wind will take it."

Freddie lifted the kite. To his delight, it went up quickly, darting through the air until he had a hard time holding on to the cord. A strong gust snatched it from his hand, but Mr. Bobbsey grabbed the string just in time. After a little practice, the young kite fliers were able to manage by themselves.

"Have fun," Mrs. Bobbsey said as she and her husband headed back to the house.

However, it wasn't long before the wind grew strong and blustery again. For the second time, it almost whipped Freddie's kite out of his grasp.

"Wait, I'll help you," Bert shouted from across the field where he was playing with his kite. He tied it to a nearby fence and ran to his brother.

"You need more weight on the tail," Bert said. "I'll tie a stone to it."

As he looked at the ground for one of a suitable size, Flossie cried out, "There goes your kite, Bert. Did you put a stone or something on it?"

"Huh?"

Puzzled, Bert gazed up at the soaring kite. There was something black hanging from the end.

Freddie gulped in horror. "It's Snoop!"

▪ 6 ▪

Ghost Warning

"Oh, please save Snoop!" Freddie begged Bert.

Nan, in the meantime, heard someone laughing and shot a glance at the fence.

"Danny Rugg!" she fumed, racing toward him. "Did you tie the kite around our cat?" Her brown eyes blazed.

"It won't hurt him. He'll have a nice ride!"

"You're the meanest boy I've ever known!" she declared, and ran back to join the others.

They were aghast as the kite bounced over the ground, dragging Snoop with it. Freddie and Flossie began to cry. At last the cord snapped and the animal landed at the edge of the field.

The children darted after him.

"Come here, Snoop!" Freddie called.

But the cat had vanished in the tall grass.

"He's going away," Flossie said, running as fast as her chubby legs could carry her.

"He'll come back!" Danny shouted.

Nan turned and glowered at him. "He'd better," she said.

Suddenly she saw a curve of black fur behind a mound of rock and signaled the other children to stop. She watched for a moment, then moved forward. Snoop arched his back slightly, which made Nan hesitate.

"She'll catch him," Freddie told Flossie.

"I hope so."

The older girl edged closer now. Her strides were long and careful. They brought her within inches of the cat. However, as she took one last step, the grass crunched under her feet, and Snoop flew out of hiding. Nan dived after him, reaching for his tail. But it slid right through her fingers.

"Oh, no!" the twins groaned, watching their pet dodge past a big tree.

Bert and the others caught up to Nan. She was as mystified as they were. Where had he gone?

"He's never coming back," Flossie said, rubbing her eyes.

Freddie kicked the grass with his heel.

Then from somewhere overhead they heard mewing.

"You're wrong," Nan said. She looked up at

the tree. Snoop was perched on the lowest limb.

"Come down, Snoop!" Freddie said while the cat licked his paw.

"Come down, pretty please!" Flossie chorused.

By now Bert had a foothold on the trunk of the tree and pulled himself up. Snoop leapt to another, smaller branch. It started to break, making the cat slide to the ground right in front of the children. This time he was completely surrounded, and Freddie grabbed him. He stroked Snoop gently.

"Were you afraid?" Flossie asked, putting her curly head close to look into the kitten's eyes.

Snoop sneezed and shook his head.

"You're a brave kitty!" the little girl exclaimed.

Later, at lunch, the twins told their mother and father about Danny's trick and how Snoop had run away. Then the talk turned to the old Marden house. Since it was Saturday, Bert and Freddie decided it would be a good time to search the place again.

"Do you want to go with us?" Bert asked the girls.

"No, we've already made plans to have a cookie sale," Nan said. "We've just got to raise some money for the new gym, although—"

She and Flossie were tempted to put the sale off.

"Do you want to go with us or not?" Bert asked again.

Nan shook her head firmly. "We can't," she said. "I made a promise."

"You made two promises. You made one to Mrs. Marden, too," Bert answered.

Nan curled her lower lip. "I know," she said, feeling guilty. "Good luck anyway," she told the boys.

The school building was deserted, and somehow the quiet made the empty old house seem more mysterious than ever.

"It really looks scary, doesn't it, Bert?" Freddie remarked.

"Oh, you think so?" his brother said, trying to act assured. "It's just an abandoned house."

"Are we going inside?" Freddie asked.

"That's why we're here." The older boy took the key from his pocket. "Maybe we can find some clue to the missing treasure."

The pair had almost reached the sagging porch, when they heard an eerie moan from above. Freddie halted. "D-did you hear that?" he stuttered.

Bert took a deep breath, keeping his nerves under control. "Yes, I did."

"What is it?" the young twin whispered.

Hushing him, the other boy waited and listened. From above they heard a loud rattling sound.

"Look!" Freddie said, pointing to the side of the house. A shutter in a second-floor window slowly swung open, then crashed shut.

"Stay away from this house!" a raspy voice warned. It was coming from behind the closed window blind.

"Come on. Let's go!" the small twin pleaded.

But his brother did not budge. "Whoever he is, he isn't supposed to be there. We're going in and see who it is!"

"Do you really think we should?" Freddie quavered.

On second thought Bert decided that perhaps it wasn't such a good idea to take the boy into the house.

"I'll tell you what," Bert said under his breath. "We'll pretend to go away, then sneak back and watch the house to see if anyone comes out."

Freddie was relieved. "That's a great idea!" He cleared his throat and said in a loud voice, "I'm going home, Bert."

"Okay. Me, too," his brother replied in an equally loud voice.

The two boys walked off. Once out of sight of the house, they scooted around the school building and circled back, approaching the old mansion from the other side. Here they found a crumbling stone wall covered with vines.

Bert pulled Freddie down behind the wall. "We can see both the front and the back of the house from here," he said.

The boys sat on the ground, making themselves as comfortable as possible, and fixed their eyes on the old house. In a little while Freddie grew restless.

"I don't think anybody will ever come out," he said, puffing his cheeks and letting the air out slowly. "Can't we go home?"

Bert nudged his brother. The back door was opening. In a moment a man had crept outside and bolted through the hedge at the rear of the property.

The older boy jumped to his feet. "We have to tell Mr. Tetlow!"

"But he isn't at school today!" Freddie reminded him.

"We'll call him at home."

The boys ran to a candy store across the street from the school. In the back of the store was a pay phone. Bert quickly called information and got Mr. Tetlow's home phone number. It took less than a minute for the principal to come on the line and for Bert to relate what had happened.

"I'll be right over," Mr. Tetlow said.

Soon they were all headed for the Marden house.

"I wonder how the man got in," Bert said.

"That's a real puzzler," the principal replied. "There are supposed to be only two keys to this house. I have one and you have the other!"

He took out his key and opened the front door. Except for the echo of their own footsteps down the hall, everything was quiet.

"We'll look through all the rooms and check the window locks as we go," Mr. Tetlow said, turning into the room to the right of the entrance.

Now that a grown-up was with them, Freddie felt very brave. He circled the room and examined every window bolt. All of them were securely fastened. The same thing was true in the other rooms on the first floor.

When the searchers reached the second floor, however, they found two broken windows. "No one could possibly get in here without a ladder," Mr. Tetlow commented.

"I didn't see one outside," Bert offered.

"Then we don't need to worry about these windows," Mr Tetlow assured him.

Returning to the first floor, he bolted the back door on the inside. "No one will be able to open this door now!" he stated firmly. "Let's go down to the cellar. Where are the stairs?"

All of a sudden Bert looked startled. "Come to think of it, I don't remember seeing any," he said.

"What about the trapdoor that Nan saw?" Freddie asked.

"We couldn't find any way to open it."

"Show me where it is," Mr. Tetlow said. "Maybe I can figure it out."

Bert led the way to the kitchen and pointed out the cracks in the floor where they had seen the trapdoor. Mr. Tetlow got down on his knees and carefully examined the old boards.

He motioned to the boys shortly. "See these two little holes?" he said. "I think at one time a handle was inserted here. I may be able to pry up these boards."

He took out a pocketknife and opened a screwdriver attachment. He pushed it into the crack nearest the holes and used it as a lever. The board raised a little.

"I can get hold of it now!" Bert exclaimed. He placed the tips of his fingers at the edge of the board and pulled. It came up slowly, revealing a flight of rickety-looking steps leading down into darkness.

"I thought we might need a flashlight," Mr.

Tetlow said, "so I brought one from the car."

He pulled it out of his pocket and, flashing it ahead of him, descended the steps. Bert and Freddie followed eagerly. When they reached the bottom, they glanced in every direction. As their eyes adjusted to the gloom they could see more of the cellar from the light that seeped through a dirty window.

The floor and walls were made of unevenly spaced bricks. The ceiling was so low that the principal was forced to stoop as he went to the windows. Glass was missing from the second window, but in its place was a wide board that had been wedged into the frame.

"That's strange. There are windows only on one side," Bert mused.

He trod slowly around the edge of the cellar and felt the opposite wall. One section was covered with wood and cobwebs. To his utter amazement, as he touched it, the wall started to move! With a creak it jerked and slid to one side!

"It's a secret entrance!" Bert cried.

■ 7 ■

The Chimney Clue

Mr. Tetlow and Freddie ran to Bert's side. "You must have touched a hidden spring!" the school principal said.

"But why would Mrs. Marden have a secret entrance to her cellar?" Freddie asked.

"I doubt that she put it in." Mr. Tetlow laughed.

His answer perplexed Bert greatly. "Then who did?"

"I don't know, but chances are it was done by the original owner. Many of these old places had secret entrances for runaway slaves from the South."

Mr. Tetlow inspected the sliding wall.

"What are we going to do about it?" Bert asked.

"Nothing at the moment. It isn't likely anyone knows about the sliding door. Since the house is going to be torn down soon anyway, we won't worry about it."

Bert closed the secret door, and the three went up into the kitchen again. As Mr. Tetlow strode to the front door, he said, "I'll notify the police that there has been another intruder here and ask them to keep a watch on the house."

As the boys walked home, Freddie said, "Maybe it was the same man you saw yesterday."

"Maybe," Bert replied, "but whoever it was won't be able to come in that back door again!"

When he and Freddie reached home, they found the rest of the family ready to sit down to supper. They hurried to wash their hands and faces.

"How was the cookie sale?" Bert asked, sliding into a chair.

"Fine," Nan said without much enthusiasm. "How did things go at the Marden house?"

"Bert found a secret entrance!" Freddie announced.

"I wish I'd been there," the older girl said glumly.

"Me, too," Flossie added.

"You could've come, if you wanted to," Bert said.

"I know." Nan picked at the carrots on her plate.

"Tell us about the secret entrance, Bert," their mother interrupted.

Bert and Freddie described the cellar of the old house and how Bert had discovered the sliding door.

"I'll bet whoever lifted that trapdoor in the kitchen came in through the secret entrance," Nan said, perking up.

"No one has touched that in years," her brother disagreed. "It was covered with cobwebs."

"I want to see the secret door!" Flossie declared. "Will you show it to me, Freddie?"

Bert answered instead. "We'll show you and Nan on Monday, but you can't tell anyone about it."

"'Cause the sliding door can still be opened," Freddie chimed in.

"I like secrets!" Flossie said.

"Mrs. Marden is coming to dinner tomorrow," Mrs. Bobbsey interjected. "You might ask her about the cellar door."

"Maybe she remembers where she put the cameo and coins," Nan said hopefully.

The next afternoon was chillier than it had been, but the sky was cloudless as Mr. Bobbsey drove the twins out to the Rolling Acres Retirement Home.

"There she is!" Flossie said as they swung in front of the main entrance. Mrs. Marden was waiting just inside and waved through the glass door.

She was wearing a robin's-egg-blue coat over a matching blue-and-white-print dress. As she got into the car, the twins noticed something else, too—a small pin on her collar.

"You found it!" Flossie said, her blue eyes wide as saucers.

"Found what, dear?" Mrs. Marden asked, smiling at Flossie.

"Your cameo!" The little girl pointed to her collar.

For a moment Mrs. Marden looked confused. "Oh, my pin. My husband brought it from Italy before we were married. I've always worn it." She shook her head sadly. "No, I haven't found the antique one yet. That was set with diamonds."

Seeing how upset she was, Mr. Bobbsey quickly changed the subject, and nothing more was said about the lost articles.

Later, when Dinah brought in a towering strawberry shortcake for dessert, Bert mentioned their recent discovery.

Mrs. Marden smiled. "My husband told me there was supposed to be a door like that, but we never found it. Lots of old houses had secret doors and cupboards, you know." She looked off in the distance. "I had a strange dream last night," she said.

"Was it a nightmare?" Freddie asked, sitting next to her.

She chucked the boy under the chin. "No. I dreamed I was walking up a chimney," she said.

Flossie giggled and said, "Maybe you were Santa Claus!"

Under the cover of laughter Bert whispered to Nan, "Maybe she hid everything in the chimney."

"That's just what I was thinking." His sister winked.

While their parents took Mrs. Marden back to Rolling Acres, the four children went into a huddle. Bert and Nan told the younger twins their latest idea.

"You mean the cameo and the coins might be in the chimney?" Freddie said.

"Well, it's a thought," Nan said.

The next day, as soon as school was over, the twins met Charlie and Nellie by the door. "Are we going to search the chimneys now?" Freddie asked.

"We've already looked at all the fireplaces,"

Nellie reminded them. "Do you think we missed something?"

Nan mentioned Mrs. Marden's dream. "Bert and I figure it could be a clue."

The six children walked to the old house, and Bert unlocked the door.

"I hope that man who keeps running away isn't in here now!" Flossie said as they went inside.

Nan took her hand. "No one can get in the house now," she said, which comforted Flossie.

Bert had brought a flashlight, which they used to explore each of the chimneys. Not a brick was loose in any of them.

"Nothing's hidden there," Bert said.

"Let's look at the sections that run through the attic," Nan suggested.

"You lead this time," Bert said.

The others agreed, and they trudged single file up the two flights of stairs. At the top they paused for another conference.

"There are four chimneys, two at each end," Bert pointed out. "We can figure out where they are and check out the walls around them."

Nan and Nellie started toward one end of the long room. Suddenly Nellie stopped. "Look!" she cried. "The trunk!"

"What's the matter?" Charlie asked. "We

looked in that trunk the last time we were here."

"But it's open," Nan said, "and I'm sure we put the lid down when we left!"

The trunk, which the children had dragged into the middle of the dusty floor, stood where they had left it. But the top was up, and the tray had not been replaced.

"I guess the mysterious intruder has been poking around the attic," Bert said.

"Do you think he's looking for Mrs. Marden's things?" Freddie asked.

Charlie laughed. "If he is, he's about as lucky as we are, and that's not very lucky."

"Let's do the chimneys," Nan said.

"Where are they?" Flossie asked. "I don't see any."

Nan explained that the chimneys ran up the outside of the house. "But Bert and I thought there might be some sort of secret cupboard or hiding place on the inside."

Bert walked to one of the windows and after a few tugs managed to open it. He leaned out and scanned the side of the house.

"The chimneys start about six feet from either side of this window," he announced, drawing his head back.

The children divided into two groups. They felt every inch of wall space behind the chimneys, then went to the opposite end of the attic and did the same thing. Once again they were disappointed.

"I guess Mrs. Marden's dream didn't mean anything," Flossie said when they were done.

"Guess not," Freddie repeated while Bert punched one hand into the other.

He and Nan had been so sure the dream was a clue. "I just wish I could think of another place to look," she said.

"Let's pull those dresses out of the trunk," Nellie suggested. "Mrs. Marden might have put her things in a pocket."

Whoever had opened the trunk had mussed up its contents considerably. Charlie and Bert looked on as the girls took the dresses out one after the other and went through all the pockets.

In one they found a lace glove with no fingers, and in another a faded dance program.

"Isn't this pretty?" Nellie exclaimed, holding up a dark-red satin dress. The material was so stiff, it stood upright when Nellie set it on the floor.

"I'm going to try it on!" Nan said. She slipped the costume over her jeans and began to parade around the attic. She held her arm high and cocked her wrist.

"Oh, your highness!" Nellie bowed and giggled.

Then she and Flossie each put on an old gown. Flossie's was so long she looked as if she were standing in a puddle of green silk. The folds spread out in soft ripples and made a swishing sound when she walked.

"Let's go downstairs," Charlie said in a bored tone. "This isn't helping us find anything."

The girls reluctantly put the costumes back in the trunk, closed the lid, and followed Bert and Charlie downstairs. When they reached the landing between the first and second floors, they heard a muffled sound below. Was it coming from the cellar?

Everyone stopped short. So did the strange, unexpected noise. But as they tiptoed down the last flight of steps, another *thump* came.

Hearts pounding, the younger twins flew to the front door and raced outside. The older children hurried after them.

They had not gone far when Bert spoke. "I forgot to lock the door. I'll have to go back."

Flossie spun toward her brother. "Oh, don't—" she began. Her eyes shifted to an upper window. "The ghost!"

The others stared. One of the shutters on the second floor had been pushed open. In the window was a white figure, swaying ominously!

■ 8 ■
Stormy Troubles

Flossie started to run, but Nan caught her by the hand. "Don't be scared, honey," she said. "Nothing is going to hurt you. There is no such thing as a ghost."

"Are you sure?" Flossie asked. Her stomach felt queasy.

"Well, *I'm* sure!" Freddie said. "That's just somebody dressed up to look like one."

"And I intend to find out who this somebody is!" Bert declared.

"If you're going into the house again, I'm going with you," Nan insisted. She glanced at Nellie and Charlie. "Will you please stay with Freddie and Flossie until we get back?"

Nellie and Charlie said they would wait for Bert and Nan. As the older twins headed toward the house, the ghostly figure in the window waved its arms and let out an unearthly screech.

Flossie begged them to come back, but the

young detectives continued on resolutely. When they reached the front door, Bert opened it noiselessly. Everything was still.

After a moment Bert whispered, "Let's go upstairs and see if the ghost is still there."

"Okay," Nan said.

Hardly daring to breathe, they crawled silently up the stairs. At the top, Bert motioned to a doorway on their right. His sister gave a nod.

Pausing after each step and hoping that the old floorboards wouldn't creak, they advanced toward the bedroom. The door was ajar, allowing them to see inside. The shapeless white figure was still facing the window. Suddenly it raised its arms in a threatening gesture.

With a stifled squeal, Nan pointed to the ghost's feet. It was wearing sneakers and orange-blue-and-green socks!

Bert shot across the room, and before the ghost could escape, the boy snatched off its sheet. "Danny Rugg!" the young detective said. He squinted his eyes accusingly.

Furious, the bully whipped around. "You think you're so smart, Bert Bobbsey!" he sputtered. "But I really made you shake this time."

"You didn't make us shake at all!" Nan assured him.

"I'd like to know how you got in here!" Bert

demanded. "Mr. Tetlow gave me a key, and nobody else is supposed to come in!"

"Teacher's pet." Danny smirked. "Well, I don't need any old key."

Bert was afraid that Danny had somehow found out about the sliding door in the cellar. If so, someone else could find it, too, and perhaps steal the hidden jewelry and coins.

On the other hand, if Danny didn't know about the secret entrance, Bert didn't want to mention it and give away the secret.

Nan guessed her twin's dilemma. "You might as well stop playing tricks on us, Danny. You didn't scare us a bit," she said, walking away, "not one little bit."

Bert trailed after her. Crestfallen, Danny picked up his sheet and left also. Once outside, he ran the other way toward his home.

"We just saw Danny come out of the house," Charlie said.

"And did he look mad," Nellie added.

Nan's eyes danced in merriment. She told the story of the "ghost" in the checkered socks, making her listeners double over with laughter.

"The latest style for ghosts!" Charlie exclaimed.

When the Bobbseys reached home, they ran inside to tell their mother about their "spooky" adventure, and also their failure to find anything.

"Perhaps you ought to give up the search," Mrs. Bobbsey advised. "Mrs. Marden may not have hidden anything in the house."

"But, Mommy, we can't give up now!" Flossie persisted.

The Bobbseys had no luck all week. On Friday, Nellie invited the girls to her house for supper. Freddie, who was lonesome, wandered aimlessly from his room to the den, where Bert was reading.

"Ber-errrt?" he said.

His brother put down his book. "Yeah?"

"Want to go camping tonight?"

"If you want to."

Freddie's eyes lit up. "I do!"

"We can pitch a tent down by the lake. Maybe Charlie will go with us."

The boys discussed the idea with their parents, who gave their permission readily. Next Bert called Charlie. In minutes he appeared with his sleeping bag.

The twins loved to go camping. Each one had a sleeping bag, and they owned several tents. From the attic Bert brought down a pup tent and two sleeping bags.

Dinah added to the pile of equipment a package of frankfurters, a can of baked beans, a package of buns, a box of cookies, and a large thermos of juice.

"If you're going to camp on the lake shore near the lumberyard," Mr. Bobbsey said, "Sam can drive you. He has to deliver some lumber in Dalton, so he can drop you off on his way."

Dinah's husband, Sam Johnson, was Mr. Bobbsey's foreman. Tall and sturdy like Dinah, he rubbed his head when he saw what the boys intended to take.

"Looks like an awful lot of equipment for one night," he teased.

Freddie's cheeks dimpled in a smile. He helped his brother put the bags in the truck while Charlie got into the cab next to Sam. Soon they were driving along the shore of Lake Metoka, where Sam pulled over to let them out.

"Need any help?" he asked before leaving.

The boys thanked him but said they could manage.

"The first thing to do is set up the tent," Bert directed. They carried their supplies to a little clearing among the trees.

"We ought to find level ground," Charlie added.

Freddie ran to an area near the water. "Here's a good place," he called.

The two older boys carried over the tent.

They drove the two poles into the sandy earth and stretched the tent over the connecting rope. Freddie helped pound in the pegs. Then they tied the tent ropes to the pegs.

"All done!" Freddie chortled.

"Now let's build a fire so we can cook supper," Bert said. He started to gather small pieces of driftwood from the beach.

Freddie and Charlie helped until they had a small pile of wood. They put stones around it. Then Charlie crumpled the paper bag that had held the thermos and stuffed it down among the twigs. He lit a match to it and watched the flames grow into a nice crackling fire.

"I'll get some sticks for the hot dogs and sharpen them," Bert said.

Charlie busied himself opening the can of beans. He dumped them into a small saucepan and held it over the fire. The aroma of cooking food swirled quickly through the air, making the boys extremely hungry.

In no time at all they had downed the frankfurters and beans. By the time they had cleaned up the remains of the meal, it was dark—almost pitch-black, in fact—and Freddie crawled into his sleeping bag. The other two crawled into theirs, and soon all was quiet inside the tent.

But a while later the little boy was awakened

by a rustling noise outside. It sounded as if something was being dragged along the ground. He raised his head cautiously and peered out of the tent. All he could see were two shiny black balls staring at him!

"Bert!" he whispered. "Wake up!" He pulled at his brother's sleeping bag.

"What is it?" Bert murmured sleepily and rolled over.

"Bert!" Freddie called again.

This time the boy sat up. "Wha-aat?"

Freddie pointed to the eyes, motionless at the tent entrance. Bert picked up his flashlight, which he had placed nearby, and shone it into the darkness. The light fell on a little animal with brownish-gray fur and a black stripe across the eyes that looked like a mask.

"A raccoon!" Bert exclaimed, sending the intruder into the darkness. "He was probably looking for something to eat. Go back to sleep."

"'Night," Freddie said. He snuggled down into his sleeping bag again.

It seemed to Bert that only a few minutes had passed, when the tent began to shake from a strong wind and he could hear the pounding of waves on the lake shore.

Then the wind howled, waking the others,

71

too. Through the tent opening they could see trees bending under the gale force.

"The tent's going down!" Freddie cried.

The boys scrambled out of their bags and dashed to the tent pegs. They struggled to push them deeper into the ground, but it was too late. The rain was beating down hard.

At the same time, a streak of lightning and a loud thunderclap awakened the rest of the Bobbsey family at home.

"We'd better get the boys," Mr. Bobbsey said to his wife. She was already putting on her boots.

"Those poor kids," she said as they finally pulled out of the driveway. "They're probably soaked by now."

"I'll take the back road. It's a little shorter," her husband said worriedly.

As he drove, the downpour made it difficult for him to see very far ahead. From time to time branches cracked off the trees and crashed onto the road.

Finally Mr. and Mrs. Bobbsey reached the lumberyard and turned down the narrow road to the lake.

The rain pelted hard against the windshield. "I can't see a thing, Dick!" his wife said.

Mr. Bobbsey turned on his high beams. They

shone onto the lake. "The tent's in the water!" he said.

Watching the canvas bob further and further away, the twins' mother panicked.

When the rain had hit the campers, Freddie, Bert, and Charlie had worked frantically to steady the pegs. But the wind was much too strong. A violent gust lifted the canvas high into the air. The tent sailed out across a sliver of sandy beach and into the lake!

The trio dashed to the edge of the shoreline. But the tent had floated out of their reach.

"We'll have to let it go," Bert said. "Maybe we can get it tomorrow."

"Now what are we going to do?" Freddie asked. Water dripped from his hair and face, and his clothes clung to his tiny frame.

Bert picked up his soggy sleeping bag. "I guess we'd better walk home," he answered.

The other two boys shouldered their gear as well and they all started off, slipping and sliding on the muddy path. Suddenly they found themselves blinded by the glare of headlights.

As they stopped, a familiar voice shouted over the noise of the truck engine, "Get in!"

"Sam!" Freddie cried, sloshing up to the open door. "Am I glad to see you!"

"I was just on my way back from Dalton," Sam

said as the boys got in. "When the rain started, I thought I'd better see how you were doing."

"The tent blew away," Bert said.

"Well, just so long as *you* didn't," Sam responded.

As the truck rolled on through the storm, the campers gazed at the deserted streets of Lakeport.

"I can just about see the school," Bert remarked.

"This rain's mean, all right," Sam said.

Charlie pressed his nose against the side window. "Isn't that a light in the Marden house?"

"I don't see any," Bert replied, leaning forward to get a better look.

"Sure there is, Bert," Freddie said. "It's in the kitchen!"

"Danny wouldn't be there in the middle of the night," his brother muttered to himself.

"What do you mean, 'middle of the night'? It's four in the morning!" Sam said. He slowed the truck, and they all gazed at the old mansion.

"There *is* a light in the kitchen," Charlie went on. "And it's flickering like a candle."

■ 9 ■
A Muddy Puzzle

As the group watched the flickering light in the Marden house, Bert urged, "Let's see who's there."

Sam put his foot on the accelerator. "No, you don't. Not while I'm here!" he said, and sped toward Charlie's house.

"I'll call the police as soon as I get in," Charlie promised, "and tell them about the light."

When the truck pulled up in front of his house, the lights were on. Mr. Mason ran down the walk. "I just called the Bobbseys, and Nan told me your parents were going to pick you up."

Sam explained about his late delivery trip, adding, "Mr. and Mrs. Bobbsey are probably back home by now."

The twins' parents, however, were still searching vigorously for the three campers.

"Maybe they've taken shelter among the trees," Mr. Bobbsey said, getting out of the car as the rain slackened. He took a flashlight from the glove compartment.

His wife pushed through the underbrush behind him and called their names, but to no avail. "They could've started walking home," Mr. Bobbsey said, going back to the car.

But they passed no one on the main road back to their house.

"I think we should call the police," Mrs. Bobbsey told her husband.

As they turned up their driveway, however, Sam Johnson appeared at the back door, and Mr. Bobbsey rolled down his car window. "They're home!" Sam shouted.

Bert and Freddie, standing in their bathrobes, waved from the kitchen.

"Oh, thank goodness," Mrs. Bobbsey said.

Inside, Nan and Flossie had set the breakfast table while Dinah fixed bowls of hot cereal for everyone. She explained that she had been asleep in the couple's cottage behind the Bobbsey house, and the sound of Sam's truck had awakened her. She had heard the children's voices outside and immediately got up to investigate.

"Dinah's a detective, too!" Freddie said with a laugh as he finished his cereal.

"We can still get a few hours' sleep," Mr. Bobbsey said, noting the time.

As they started upstairs, Bert took his father aside. He told him about the flickering light in the Marden mansion. "Charlie was going to call the police as soon as he got home," the boy remarked, barely able to keep his eyes open.

"When you wake up, we'll find out all about it," his father replied. He patted the boy on the shoulder. "Good night, son."

"Good night, Dad." Bert yawned.

At the first crack of sunshine, the twins reconvened in the kitchen. Freddie described their camping adventure in more detail while his brother kept watch on the telephone.

"C'mon, Charlie, call us," he said, blinking as the front doorbell rang. "That's him!" He dashed into the hallway as Mr. Bobbsey answered it.

"Good morning, Officer Murphy," he said, opening the door wide. "What brings you here?"

The policeman told him about Charlie Mason's call.

"Did you find the intruder?" Bert asked.

"Unfortunately, no," Officer Murphy replied. "Our men got a key from Mr. Tetlow and searched the house, but no one was there."

Seeing the disappointed looks on all the children's faces, the officer added, "Our men did find some muddy footprints on the kitchen floor. So we know someone was there."

The older twins looked at each other in amazement. Who was the intruder? How had he entered the house? And *why* was he there?

"Do you think someone is living in the place?" Nan asked.

"I doubt it. We would have found some evidence," Murphy explained. "We'll patrol the house round the clock and let you know if we catch anyone."

After he had left, Nan said, "I have a hunch someone else knows about Mrs. Marden's lost treasure."

"I hope he doesn't find it!" Flossie said.

That afternoon the twins elected to go through the old house once more.

"If only we had one clue!" Nan sighed.

Before they left home, they phoned Mrs. Marden. "I'm so glad to hear from you," the woman said. "I've been trying to remember where I could have possibly hidden those things." She paused. "Just before I moved from the house, I was out in the yard burning some trash, and I'm sure I had the cameo and the box of coins in my pocket at the time."

"Do you think you burned them?" Nan asked, feeling a new wave of despair.

Mrs. Marden's voice trembled. "I hope not, dear. Perhaps you children should check the backyard. I've searched all my pockets, and my precious, precious heirlooms aren't in them."

Later, as the twins related the story to their mother, Dinah overheard them. "I'm sorry to add to your problems," she said, "but I've been calling and calling to Snoop. I don't know where he is. He hasn't been around all day."

"Snoop wouldn't run away again," Freddie said.

But although the children looked under the shrubbery and in the trees, they couldn't find the cat.

"Wait a minute," Nan said. "Maybe—"

"What is it?" Freddie asked.

"Maybe he went back to Taylor's! That was his home before he came here."

Flossie jumped up and down. "Let's go!" she said.

Mrs. Bobbsey offered to drive the children downtown. "I'll stay in the car while you ask about Snoop," she said, parking near the entrance.

"Okay," Flossie replied. She hurried after the other twins.

When they finally reached the shipping room, Freddie discovered the watchman just arriving. "Hi, Mr. Ryan," Freddie said. "Has Snoop come back?"

"Well, hello there." He smiled at the visitors. "Now, who is Snoop?"

"He's the black cat you gave me."

Mr. Ryan sat back in his chair and scratched his head. "Oh, of course. Did he run away?"

Nan explained that Snoop had disappeared. She thought he might have returned to the store.

"Sorry," the man said. "He hasn't been here."

Disappointed, his listeners headed for the escalator. Instantly Nan had another thought. She ran back to the shipping room. "Excuse me, Mr. Ryan, but was Snoop always your cat?" she inquired.

"Well, no, as a matter of fact. He belonged to a woman who used to shop here frequently. I hadn't seen her for a long time. Then one day she came in again. She said she was getting rid of her house and didn't know what to do with her cat. I like company when I'm here at night, so I offered to take him."

"Maybe Snoop went to her house," Nan surmised. "Do you know where she lived?"

"Afraid not. She brought the cat in and left it. I never did ask her name."

Nan began to leave again, when another thought occurred to her. "What did this woman look like?" she asked Mr. Ryan.

The woman he described sounded just like Mrs. Marden!

Nan excitedly told the others what she had found out.

"A cat likes to go back to his first home," said Bert. "So if Snoop did belong to Mrs. Marden, he could be at the old house now!"

Mrs. Bobbsey dropped the children off at the Marden house. "Don't stay too long," she cautioned.

"We won't," Bert replied.

The four children searched the house, but there was no Snoop. Then they went out to the backyard, which was about the same size as their own. It was bordered by a tall hedge that grew at the end and along one side. On the opposite side was a small toolshed, and beyond it stretched an open field. They searched for Snoop everywhere.

"Well, as long as we're here, we might as well look for the jewelry and coins," Bert proposed.

They looked all around the shed's rickety steps and under the sagging structure. Then Freddie ran to the hedge. He picked up a stout stick and began to dig at the roots. Flossie took another stick and went to help him.

"I've found something," Flossie announced shortly, jabbing at the soil.

But as Bert and Nan scraped away the dirt, they discovered it was only a red brick.

Nan strolled across the yard and stopped in front of the toolshed. "Look at this," she called out.

When the others joined her, Nan pointed to an area of lawn that was bare except for bits of glass and wisps of half-charred cloth. "This must be where Mrs. Marden burned her trash," she said.

Bert bent down and sifted through the debris carefully. "I don't think the cameo would burn," he said, "and certainly not the coins. Part of them might melt, but I'm sure there'd be something left."

"Any signs?" Nan asked, crouching beside her twin.

"Nope."

The young detectives looked at the ashes but found nothing that remotely resembled the cameo or any kind of metal. Next they checked all the forks of the trees within reach and searched the ground for evidence of fresh digging.

"Well, I guess the toolshed is the only place we haven't looked," Bert said finally.

But the little house was too small for all four children to stand in at one time. It was decided that Freddie and Flossie would go in first. The space around the edge of the floor was filled with cans and buckets of dried-up paint, and on the wall hung rusty garden tools covered with cobwebs.

Freddie picked his way through the junk to the back wall. Attached to it was a low shelf.

"Here's something!" he said, spying a little box on top. He stretched his arms and took hold of it. "It rattles!" he exclaimed.

As Freddie carried his discovery outside, his twin sister jumped up and down. "I think you've found the treasure!" she said.

■ 10 ■
Two Snoops

Bert and Nan watched breathlessly as Freddie pried up the lid of the old cigar box. Seeing the contents, they groaned in unison.

"I don't believe it! Bolts and screws!" Bert said disgustedly.

This second disappointment was too much for Flossie. "I'm tired," she said, looking forlorn.

"We might as well go home," the older boy agreed.

"I guess so," Nan sighed. "There's nothing more to do here." She put her arm around Freddie's shoulder and followed Bert and Flossie out of the yard.

The young sleuths hardly said anything all evening, which troubled Mr. and Mrs. Bobbsey.

"May we phone Mrs. Marden?" Nan asked. "Maybe Snoop wasn't her cat after all."

"Can you wait till tomorrow?" Mrs. Bobbsey

said. "I don't think we ought to disturb Mrs. Marden so late. I'm going to take some books to Mrs. Marden in the afternoon. Who would like to go with me?"

"I would," Nan and Flossie chimed in together.

"I would, too," Bert replied, "but Freddie and I want to look for our tent. We didn't have time yesterday. Sam said he'd help us."

The following day, as arranged, Sam drove the boys to the lake while Mrs. Bobbsey took Nan and Flossie to the retirement home. When they arrived, they found Mrs. Marden in the lounge. She was seated in a great wing chair with an unopened magazine on her lap. As she rose absentmindedly to greet them, it slid to the floor.

"Oh, how clumsy of me," the woman said. Nan dashed to retrieve it while her mother presented the books.

"We're working on a new mystery," Flossie revealed.

"You are?" Mrs. Marden said.

"Our cat has disappeared."

"Oh, I'm sorry to hear that. I had a cat once, a beautiful black one. I was very fond of him, but when I moved I had to give him away."

"Did you give him to friends of yours?" Nan asked.

"Oh, no. My friends have all either died or moved to places like this. I gave him to that nice man at the store where I used to shop."

The young detectives were excited. Their hunch was right. Snoop had been Mrs. Marden's cat! They told Mrs. Marden about Freddie's experience at Taylor's and how Snoop had become their cat.

"But now he's lost!" said Flossie with a pout.

When the girls arrived home, Bert and Freddie were busily spreading their wet tent on the lawn to dry. Nan shared the latest information.

"That's terrific!" Bert answered. "Maybe Snoop will turn up at the Marden house, after all!"

"Why don't we go there tomorrow," Nan said, "before school starts?"

The next morning the twins went directly to the Marden house. The Bobbseys ran through the yard, calling, "Here, kitty, kitty!" Afterward they paused to listen for an answering meow. But none came.

"I thought we were going inside," Freddie said.

Bert glimpsed the crowd of children entering the school. "It's getting late. We'd better come back this afternoon."

The day seemed longer than usual as the twins waited for the school bell to ring. When it did at long last, they met outside again.

"I told everybody about Snoop," Freddie said, "even Danny."

Bert frowned. "He's the last person I'd tell."

"But he might see Snoop," Freddie said defensively. He followed his brother to the front door of the house next door. "Did I make a big mistake? Huh, Bert?"

"You can't do much about it now." Freddie pursed his lips while Bert took out the key and fed it into the lock. "We'd better check all the closets," he said.

"And any small spaces," Nan added as they all went inside. "Anyplace a cat might crawl into."

The twin detectives explored the house quickly, but, to their dismay, there was no sign of Snoop.

"There's still the attic," Bert remarked. He and Nan trudged up the narrow stairs to the top of the house.

Freddie and Flossie, however, did not want to go. They ran down to the first floor and chased each other through the big musty rooms. Suddenly they heard a loud *meow*. They stopped running. The sound came again!

"I think it's in the living room," Flossie whispered to her brother.

The two children stepped across the hall on tiptoe. There was no cat in sight. Then they heard another loud *meow,* followed by a snicker. The sound had come from the other side of a shuttered window.

"That wasn't a cat!" the little girl declared.

She drew toward the window and peeked through the blind, then beckoned to Freddie. The twins giggled and let out a loud *meow*.

Suddenly there was a scrambling noise under the window. Through the shutter the twins saw Danny Rugg fleeing toward the school.

"He was trying to make us think he was Snoop, but we scared him!" Freddie said, grinning, as Bert came into the room.

"Find anything?" he asked.

"Only Danny," Flossie said, explaining what the boy had done.

"I'll never tell him anything again," Freddie declared.

"We ought to play a trick on him," Bert muttered angrily. "In fact, I—"

Before he could finish the sentence, Nan's voice interrupted. "Hey, everybody, come into the kitchen!" she called.

She was standing in the middle of the room, waving a paper. "What do you think of this?" she said.

"It's the last school assembly program!" Bert exclaimed. "How did that get in here?"

"Beats me," Nan replied.

Bert passed the paper to Freddie. "Look!" he said. "There's a drawing on it."

"There is? Where?" Nan asked. She studied the program closely. "It's a plan of this house." She handed it back to her twin.

"It *is* a plan," he said. "Somebody at school must have been in here! But who?"

"Danny?" Flossie suggested.

"Since we caught him in the attic? I doubt it," Nan said.

Freddie told her about the bully's latest trick, adding, "But he was outside the house."

"Well, the only other person with a key is Mr. Tetlow," Bert said. "We ought to show him this program tomorrow."

"Are we going to play a trick on Danny too?" Freddie inquired.

"*Are* we!" His brother's eyes twinkled. "I can't wait!"

That evening the children worked out a plan. Flossie provided a doll's hot-water bottle and one of her stuffed animals, a furry gray kangaroo with a spacious pouch in front.

"Purr-fect!" Bert said, laughing to himself.

Before leaving home the next day, he filled the bottle with hot water and slipped it into the pouch. Then he put the kangaroo into a brown paper bag and carried it to the classroom while Nan went to Mr. Tetlow's office.

Seeing her in the outer office, he motioned to her to come in. She gave him the program.

"I found this at the Marden house," she said as the principal glanced at the paper. "Do you have any idea who could have left it or why there is a map of the house on it?"

"I haven't been there for a week or so," he said. "This is very disturbing. I must turn this paper over to the police right away." He noted the time on a wall clock. "The bell is about to ring. You'd better go."

Nan excused herself and hurried to her classroom. As she sat down at her desk, Bert winked and made an "OK" signal. Nan tried not to look at Danny, who sat across the aisle.

"Good morning, boys and girls," Ms. Vandermeer said. "Please take out your notebooks and pencils."

Bert and Nan stared at Danny as he put his hand into his desk.

▪ 11 ▪

The Big Discovery

"Ouch!" Danny yelled, and slammed down his desk lid.

A wave of laughter flowed through the room.

Ms. Vandermeer, a slim woman with hazel eyes, which now looked fiery green, zeroed in on Danny. "What happened?" she asked sternly.

"I—uh—I stuck my finger," Danny answered, his face a deep red.

"I'm sorry if you hurt yourself," the teacher remarked, "but please don't make so much noise. Now, take out your notebook and pencil."

The troubled boy did not move. He stared straight ahead at the empty chalkboard.

"Danny! *What* is the matter with you?" the teacher continued, rushing toward him.

He gulped miserably. "I—I think there's an animal in my desk!" he finally stuttered.

"An animal!" the teacher gasped in astonishment. "Well, take it out!"

With great reluctance Danny put his hand inside and slowly removed the kangaroo. He flushed scarlet again as the class burst into roars of laughter. Even Ms. Vandermeer couldn't keep from joining in.

"I didn't put it there!" Danny cried. He pointed at Bert. "I'll bet he did."

"*Did* you, Bert?" the teacher asked.

The boy looked sheepish. "Yes, Ms. Vandermeer," he confessed. "Danny's always playing tricks on me and my brother and sisters, so I thought I'd play one on him."

"The classroom is no place for this," came the cold reply. But a little smile crossed her lips. "I will keep the stuffed animal in my desk until noontime. You may pick it up then. Now, let's get back to work."

With a few suppressed giggles the students bent over their notebooks.

Shortly before noon a message came for Bert and Nan to report to the principal's office. "I wonder if he's going to punish me," Bert said as they walked down the hall.

"I don't think so. I mean, why would he want to see me, too?" his sister said.

As Nan suspected, the principal did not mention the kangaroo incident. Instead, he indicated a roughly dressed man who was standing nearby with Officer Murphy.

"I thought you'd like to see who has been breaking into the Marden house," Mr. Tetlow said to the twins.

"Mr. Ringley?" Bert said, puzzled. Jack Ringley had been the school janitor until a few days ago.

"Yes," said Mr. Tetlow. "We released him when we found out he was taking our supplies. He overheard you telling your friends about Mrs. Marden's lost valuables and decided to go after them himself."

"How did he get in?" Bert questioned.

The prisoner shifted uneasily.

"That's what I wanted to know," Mr. Tetlow said. "Ringley has confessed that he took the key from my desk drawer one day when the office was empty. He had a duplicate made so he could go into the house anytime he wanted to. He returned the key before I had a chance to notice it was missing."

Officer Murphy spoke up. "We've been watching that house day and night. This morning I saw all of you leave. Then a little while later this guy walked up and let himself in with a key."

"So he didn't know about the secret entrance in the cellar!" Nan exclaimed in satisfaction.

Ringley was about to talk but caught himself.

"Did you know about the trapdoor in the kitchen?" the boy detective asked him. "Were you the one who used it when we were in the house?"

"So what?" the man answered snidely. "You almost caught me. I had to duck down when I heard her"—he nodded at Nan—"coming toward the kitchen."

"What about the lower step? You removed that, too, right?" Bert accused.

"I wanted to scare you kids so you wouldn't hang around. I had work to do that day." He sneered, adding resentfully, "I yelled at you from the upstairs window, but it didn't do any good!"

"You must have looked in the trunk in the attic. Did you find anything?" Nan inquired.

The man grumbled in disgust, "A lot of old dresses!"

The former janitor confessed that he had even gone into the house late one night to search for the heirlooms. But again he had had no luck.

"That must have been the night Sam drove us home from the lake!" Bert cried. "We saw a light in the kitchen."

Mr. Tetlow took the school program from his desk. "I guess you dropped this on one of your trips," he said. The prisoner looked away. "That's all," the principal went on. "The mystery of the haunted house has finally been solved!"

After the officer left with Jack Ringley, Mr. Tetlow stood up. "Well, it looks as if Mrs. Marden's valuables are never going to be found. The wreckers are to start tearing down the old place this afternoon."

"I guess her things aren't there anyway if none of us could find them," Nan concluded. She and Bert departed.

Freddie and Flossie, meanwhile, had gone home for lunch. They were waiting impatiently for the older twins when they finally came to the table.

"Where were you? How did the trick on Danny go?" Freddie asked.

"What did he do?" Flossie added.

Bert and Nan had been so excited about the capture of the mysterious intruder that they had almost forgotten about the kangaroo episode.

But now they gave a complete account. When they described how Danny's eyes had bulged upon seeing the stuffed animal and how he'd almost jumped out of his chair, Freddie and Flossie collapsed in laughter.

Dinah had stayed in the dining room to hear

the story. She clapped her hands heartily. "That boy sure got what he deserved!" she said.

"I hope this will discourage him for a while," Mrs. Bobbsey said, wiping tears of laughter from her own eyes. "But you still haven't told us why you're so late."

"The ghost in the haunted house has been caught!" Bert stated with a grin.

"Who was it?" Freddie asked.

"Tell us, tell us," Flossie said.

Bert and Nan took turns telling what had happened in Mr. Tetlow's office, which thoroughly amazed the younger twins.

"Then Danny didn't play all those tricks!" Flossie exclaimed.

"Not all of them, no," Bert admitted.

When the six-year-olds heard that the Marden house was going to be torn down that afternoon, Flossie looked sad. "But we haven't found Mrs. Marden's things yet."

"Even so, it'll be fun to watch them knock the house down," Freddie said.

That afternoon when school was dismissed, a large crowd of boys and girls gathered on the driveway to watch the housewreckers.

While one group of workmen got the machinery ready, another began tearing out woodwork that could be used again. There was a steady procession of men holding mantelpieces, fine old doors, and stair rails. These were piled into a truck and hauled away.

Finally a man climbed into the cab of a huge machine from which a crane protruded. At the end of the crane was a giant iron ball.

"That's the wrecking ball!" Freddie called out in excitement. "Watch it smash the house!"

At that moment Mr. Tetlow came from the school building and stood beside the Bobbseys. A man stationed near the house gave the signal and the huge ball swung against it.

Crash! The ball smashed into the roof and tore a big hole. Splinters of wood flew in all directions.

Then as the operator pulled the ball back for another swing, Nan Bobbsey yelled, "Stop!"

The wrecker looked from the cab of his machine. "Did someone call me?"

"I did, sir," Nan said. Followed by Mr. Tetlow and the other Bobbseys, she ran over to the huge machine. "Could you stop for a few minutes, please? I think I heard a cat crying."

"I heard it, too!" Freddie said excitedly.

"There it is again!" Bert exclaimed. "It's coming from the kitchen!"

The children and the principal hurried into the house and back to the kitchen. The logs in

the fireplace had tumbled forward and scattered on the floor. Lying on top of them was the metal-plate wall, which had also fallen inward.

Nan sped toward the opening. As she leaned to look inside, something soft jumped onto her shoulder.

It was Snoop, all covered with soot!

Freddie took the cat and held him close. "Oh, Snoop," he said, "we found you. Please don't go away again."

The animal snuggled up under the little boy's chin and purred contentedly.

"I wonder where he was." Bert pulled out his flashlight and ducked into the fireplace. "Well, I think we finally found something," he said. "That metal wall was a fake!"

▪ 12 ▪
Leading Secret

"There's another wall behind the fake one, with steps going up to the roof!" Bert said. "Snoop must have climbed to the top."

"He was probably afraid to come down, but the awful bang on the house made him," Nan concluded.

"A mystery stairway!" Freddie exclaimed. "And Snoop helped us find it!"

"The steps may lead to a secret room," Nan said. She looked at Mr. Tetlow.

"Let's go see!" Flossie proposed, starting forward.

Mr. Tetlow caught her by the hand. "Not so fast, young lady," he cautioned. "I think one of the older children should go first."

"I will," Nan volunteered. While Bert held the flashlight so that it shone in front of her, Nan went up a few steps. Suddenly she called out, "There's a box here!"

"Ooh!" Flossie cried. "Can you get it?"

Nan said no more. She backed down the steps holding a black metal container in her hands and put it on the floor. Everyone waited breathlessly while she fumbled with the clasp.

In another minute the lid was up. Inside were two small chests. One was covered in velvet, and the other was made of carved wood and had a slide top.

"Open them!" Freddie urged.

Excited, Nan pressed a little catch on the velvet case. It popped to reveal a pale green stone carved with a woman's head. The cameo was surrounded by a tiny row of sparkling diamonds!

"How bee-yoo-ti-ful!" Flossie gasped, taking the brooch from its satin bed. She held it up to the light, which made the diamonds glitter even more.

"It must be very valuable!" Mr. Tetlow exclaimed.

"Let's see what's in the other chest!" Bert said. He picked up the carved box and removed the cover. The interior was filled with square-shaped coins embossed with various figures.

"Ah! Obsidional coins!" Mr. Tetlow observed. "They're very rare."

The children took turns examining the silver pieces. One was eight-sided and bore the design of a castle with three towers. Another had an inscription in the middle and a seal in each corner.

"These are really museum pieces!" the principal said, closing the box again.

"They're Mrs. Marden's treasures," Nan said, her face glowing with pride.

"May we take them to her right away?" Flossie asked, bubbling with enthusiasm.

"I'll drive you over," Mr. Tetlow offered. He was just as eager as the twins.

When they left the old house, the principal told the wreckers to continue their work. Then he led the Bobbseys to his car. Freddie still held on tightly to Snoop. In a short while they parked in front of the Rolling Acres Retirement Home.

Flossie jumped out and ran up the walk, calling, "Mrs. Maarrrden!"

The woman came down the stairs as they entered. "What is it?" she inquired anxiously. "Is something wrong?"

"We've found your treasure! We have it right here!" Freddie shouted.

"My cat?" Mrs. Marden asked, observing the pet in his arms.

"We found him, too. But I mean your missing presents!" Flossie said. She held out the metal box.

Mrs. Marden sank into a chair. "You dear children!" she exclaimed. "Where did you find that box?"

The young detectives told the story of the wrecker and hearing the cat cry, then the discovery of the treasure in the old fireplace.

"How silly of me. Now I remember," Mrs. Marden said. "That stairway was a favorite hiding place of mine. I knew no burglar would ever think of removing the metal wall I put up. But," she continued ruefully, "I forgot that was where I had hidden the box."

Meanwhile, Snoop was straining in Freddie's arms. Finally Freddie let him go, and he jumped into Mrs. Marden's lap. "Oh, Midnight!" she exclaimed as the cat rubbed against her.

Freddie looked worried. But then Mrs. Marden said to him, "Midnight often disappeared, but I usually found him snoozing on those secret stairs. Now they're destroyed. So you will keep my pet for me, won't you?"

Freddie looked relieved and said yes eagerly. He hugged Snoop. "We all love Snoop," he said earnestly. "He's a member of our family!"

"You children are wonderful detectives," Mrs. Marden said. "You found both my treasure and my beautiful cat." She stroked him lovingly.

"Snoop found me first!" Freddie pointed out.

And he repeated the tale of his experience in the store, even though Mrs. Marden had heard it.

"Midnight is a very smart cat," she commented. Again she thanked the twins for recovering the heirlooms.

Mr. Tetlow drove the children home. When they related the day's adventures to their mother and father, Mrs. Bobbsey remarked proudly, "I told Mrs. Marden you were good at solving mysteries!"

On the way to school next morning, the twins met Charlie and Nellie.

"What happened yesterday?" Nellie asked Nan. "I saw you run into the old house, and then later you all went off with Mr. Tetlow. Charlie and I want to hear all about it!"

As quickly as they could, the twins brought their friends up-to-date on the previous day's events. "Oh, Nan, that's super!" Nellie exclaimed. "Mrs. Marden must have been thrilled!"

"You're great detectives!" Charlie praised them. Then as the group approached the school he said under his breath, "Look who's waiting for us! The Enemy!"

Danny Rugg was standing on the steps. "I hear you found your old cat," he scoffed as the Bobbseys drew nearer.

"And we're very happy about it too," Nan replied.

"He helped us solve another mystery," added Flossie.

"Now, how could a dumb cat do that?" Danny sniffed, walking away.

Bert called after him, "I'd like to know how you got into the old house."

The bully wheeled around, a smug look on his face.

"Did you have another key?" Freddie asked.

"No, I didn't have another key," Danny said, imitating the little boy. "I was in the yard the day you found that secret door in the cellar. When you left, I figured out a way to open it from the outside. So, after that, I had no trouble getting in whenever I wanted to!"

"You didn't scare us, so you were wasting your time," Bert replied.

"Which reminds me," Nan said, "I wonder how Snoop got into the house."

"Maybe he got in through a broken window," Flossie said.

"Or he could've followed the janitor in sometime," Bert suggested.

Soon the bell rang, and the children went to their classrooms. But instead of beginning the lessons, the teachers made a surprise announcement. There was to be a special assembly.

The auditorium buzzed with questions as the students filed in to take their seats. However, they grew quiet when Mr. Tetlow walked to the front of the stage.

"I have an important announcement, which I am very happy to make," he began. "I don't know whether all of you have heard about the events of yesterday afternoon. Thanks to the efforts of the Bobbsey twins," the principal continued, "some very valuable possessions of the former owner of the old house next door were found and returned to her."

Nan's face blushed a rosy pink as she caught Bert's attention in the row ahead of her. He smiled back.

As they listened to the principal tell the story of their remarkable search, the twins wondered when they would have another mystery to solve. To their amazement, the answer would come soon, during *The Bobbsey Twins' Adventure in the Country.*

Now Mr. Tetlow's speech broke into their thoughts. "Mrs. Marden is very grateful to our students," he went on, "and as an expression of her appreciation, she has asked me to sell these valuable items and to donate the proceeds to help buy equipment for our new gymnasium."

The principal's closing words brought a burst of applause and cheers from the audience.

"You did it!" Nellie said to Nan, who smiled modestly.

As the noise died down, the clear young voice of Freddie Bobbsey rose above it.

"But *we* didn't really find the treasure," he said.

"No?" Mr. Tetlow replied, acting somewhat flustered.

"Well, if you didn't, who did?" the boy next to him prodded.

"Our cat, Snoop, found it!" Freddie announced triumphantly. "He's the best detective of us all!"